BEING TEDDY ROOSEVELT

Claudia Mills

Pictures by
R. W. Alley

SQUARE
FISH

FARRAR STRAUS GIROUX
NEW YORK

To Devira Chartrand

The biography Riley reads for his report is modeled on Jean Fritz's wonderful book *Bully for You, Teddy Roosevelt!* (New York: G. P. Putnam, 1991).

SQUARE
FISH
An Imprint of Macmillan

Library of Congress Cataloging-in-Publication Data
Mills, Claudia.
Being Teddy Roosevelt / Claudia Mills ; pictures by R. W. Alley.
    p. cm.
Summary: When he is assigned Teddy Roosevelt as his biography
project in school, fourth-grader Riley finds himself inspired by
Roosevelt's tenacity and perseverance and resolves to find a way to get
what he most wants—a saxophone and music lessons.
ISBN 978-0-312-64018-7
[1. Conduct of life—Fiction.   2. Perseverance (Ethics)—Fiction.
3. Single-parent families—Fiction.   4. Friendship—Fiction.
5. Schools—Fiction.]   I. Alley, R. W. (Robert W.), ill.   II. Title.

PZ7.M63963 Bei 2007
[Fic]—dc22

                                                              2006048978

Originally published in the United States by Farrar Straus Giroux
First Square Fish Edition: January 2012
Square Fish logo designed by Filomena Tuosto
Book designed by Barbara Grzeslo
mackids.com

        10   9   8   7   6   5   4   3   2   1

AR: 4.1 / LEXILE: 670L

1

Riley gave up.

He couldn't find his language arts notebook in his desk or in his backpack. He must have forgotten it somewhere.

"Does everybody have his or her notebook ready?" Mrs. Harrow asked. "Riley?"

"I think I left it at home."

Mrs. Harrow sighed. "This is the third time this week that you're missing a notebook, Riley."

Riley was impressed that she knew the exact number of times. She remembered more about him than he remembered about himself.

Sophie sat on Riley's right. Her notebook lay open in the exact middle of her desk. The cursive on each page was as neat and beautiful as Mrs. Harrow's on the chalkboard.

Erika sat on Riley's left. She had her notebook out, but she hadn't opened it. Erika did only what she felt like doing. Apparently, she didn't feel like opening her notebook right now.

Riley's best friend, Grant, sat directly in front of Riley. His notebook was almost as perfect as Sophie's. Grant's parents bought him a video game for every A he got on his report card. Riley didn't think he could get A's even if his mother bought him ten video games for each one. He had a hard enough time getting B's and C's.

Mrs. Harrow handed Riley a piece of paper. "You can write your assignment on this."

Of course, now Riley would have to make sure he didn't lose the piece of paper.

"Don't lose it, dear," Mrs. Harrow said.

"All right, class," she went on. "We are going to be starting our fall unit on biographies. Does anyone know what a biography is?"

Sophie did. "It's a book about someone's life. A true book. About a famous person's life."

Sophie would probably have a biography written about her someday—if a person could be famous for having a neat notebook and 100 percent on every spelling test. *Sophie Sartin: The Girl Who Never Made a Mistake*. That would be the title.

Riley meant to listen to what Mrs. Harrow was saying next, but he couldn't stop thinking up titles for other biographies.

Erika Lee: The Girl Who Did What She Wanted. He noticed that Erika still hadn't opened her notebook. Mrs. Harrow hadn't said anything to her about it, either.

Grant Littleton: The Boy Who Owned Every Single Video Game System Ever Invented. Plus Every Single Game. Not a very short or snappy title, but a lot of kids would want to read that one.

What would the title of his biography be? *Riley O'Rourke: The Boy Who Couldn't Find His Notebook*. That didn't sound like a book kids would be lining up to read. *Riley O'Rourke: The Boy Who Would Forget His Head If It Weren't Fastened On.*

That's what grownups were always saying to him: "Riley, you'd forget your head if it weren't fastened on." The book would have cool illustrations, at least. There could be a picture of a seal balancing Riley's head on its nose like a beach ball. Or someone dunking his head into the hoop at a basketball game.

Riley grinned.

"Riley? Are you listening to the assignment?"

How could teachers always tell when he wasn't listening?

"Remember, class," Mrs. Harrow said, "the biography you read has to be at least one hundred pages long. Your five-page report on the biography is due three weeks from today, on Wednesday, October fourth. And then on that Friday we'll have our fourth-grade biography tea."

"What's a biography tea?" Sophie asked.

Mrs. Harrow gave the class a big smile. It was clear that she thought a biography tea was something extremely wonderful. Right away, Riley got a sinking feeling in the pit of his stomach.

"On the day of our biography tea," Mrs. Harrow said, "you will arrive at school dressed up as the subject of your biography. All day long you will act like that person. Then in the afternoon we will have a fancy tea party, and you famous people from world history will sit at special decorated tables and have tea together!"

To say that Riley would rather die than go to a biography tea would be an exaggeration. But not a big exaggeration.

Sophie gave a little squeal of delight. "I love tea parties!"

Erika gave a little snort of disgust. Riley gathered that Erika did not love tea parties.

Grant raised his hand. "We can be whoever we want, right?"

Mrs. Harrow shook her head. "Oh, no, dear. I let the children pick one year, and I got only football players and rock stars. I've prepared two hats filled with names, one for boys and one for girls. You will draw from the hats to find out the subject of your biography."

For the first time, Riley noticed two hats perched on Mrs. Harrow's desk. The black stove-

pipe Abe Lincoln hat must be for the boys. The flowered straw hat must be for the girls.

The first girl to choose got Pocahontas, an Indian princess.

The first boy to choose got Napoleon, the French emperor.

Sophie got Helen Keller, the blind and deaf woman. She didn't squeal with delight this time.

Erika got Florence Nightingale. "Who's Florence Nightingale?"

"She was a famous nurse," Mrs. Harrow said.

"I don't want to be a nurse."

"Well, dear, we all have to choose out of the hat."

"I don't want to be a nurse," Erika repeated. "I want to be someone who commands armies and rules empires and sinks ships."

"Well . . ." Riley knew Mrs. Harrow would give in. That was the only way of dealing with Erika. "I suppose you could be Queen Elizabeth the First."

Riley hoped he'd get some famous musician,

like Beethoven or Duke Ellington, or even better, a sax player like Charlie Parker.

He got President Teddy Roosevelt. That wasn't too bad. Riley had seen a picture of Teddy Roosevelt once, wearing a uniform and sitting on a horse. But reading a hundred-page book about Teddy Roosevelt and writing a five-page paper about Teddy Roosevelt and trying to drink tea while wearing a mustache would be terrible.

Grant got Mahatma Gandhi.

"Gandhi!" Grant shouted. "The bald guy who sits cross-legged on the ground in his underwear?"

"Gandhi, the great man who liberated India from the British," Mrs. Harrow corrected.

"Who liberated India from the British while sitting cross-legged on the ground in his underwear," Grant moaned.

Riley knew Grant wanted to refuse to be Gandhi. But only Erika ever refused to do things in school. Maybe Grant's parents would buy him an extra game for having to be Gandhi.

When everyone had drawn a name, Mrs. Harrow gave the class another big smile. "I can't wait for this year's biography tea!"

Riley could wait. A tea party with Pocahontas, Napoleon, Helen Keller, Queen Elizabeth I, Mahatma Gandhi, and Teddy Roosevelt?

No way!

2

Music was the last period of the school day. Riley loved it. He didn't really like to sing or do the dumb hand motions that went along with the songs. But he loved watching Mrs. Eldridge play the piano. She could play fast and loud, every note perfect, without looking at the music, without looking at the keys, and while yelling at the kids talking in the back row, all at the same time.

It was impressive, all right.

That day, another teacher was in the music room with Mrs. Eldridge, a tall man with dark hair and a big smile.

"This is Mr. Simpson," Mrs. Eldridge said. "He's the band teacher, who is here to tell you about instrumental music. Instrumental music will start for fourth graders in four weeks, meeting in the cafeteria on Tuesday and Thursday after-noons."

She sounded as excited about instrumental music as Mrs. Harrow had sounded about the bi-ography tea. But this time Riley felt excited, too.

"Do we have to do it?" Grant asked.

"No. But it's a wonderful opportunity for fourth graders to learn how to play an instru-ment."

Riley wanted to learn how to play an instru-ment. He saw that Mr. Simpson had a bunch of musical instruments laid out on a big table behind him. Riley recognized the skinny flute, and the trombone with its long slide, and the cool-looking sax.

That was the one for Riley: the sax. He had loved the sax ever since he had watched a program about Charlie Parker on TV. Now he imagined himself up on the stage, wailing away on the high notes, his fingers moving up and down the keys in a blur.

Mr. Simpson beamed at the class. "I'll let you

look at the instruments today, and you can see which one you like best."

Riley already knew he liked the saxophone best. Maybe Mr. Simpson would let them take their new instruments home today!

"How much do the instruments cost?" someone else asked.

Cost?

"If you don't want to buy an instrument right away, you can rent one," Mr. Simpson said. "Most rentals run about twenty-five dollars a month."

Riley couldn't believe it. Twenty-five dollars a month? Every month? His mother never had extra money. His dad hardly sent them any money at all.

If only someone would ask, "What if you don't have the money?" But nobody did. And Riley wasn't about to.

Mr. Simpson played a short melody on each of the instruments. They all sounded great, but the saxophone sounded greatest by far.

Riley moved closer.

Then Mr. Simpson let the kids crowd around the table to look at the instruments close up.

"First I have to be Gandhi," Grant groaned. "Now I'm going to have to play a band instrument."

"Mrs. Eldridge just said we don't have to play one," Riley reminded him.

"My parents will make me," Grant said. "And then they'll make me practice. Every time I sit down to play a video game, they'll say, 'Grant, have you practiced your instrument?' Then there will be a concert. My dad will videotape the concert. They'll show the videotape to my relatives when they come to our house. And then the relatives will say, 'Grant, why don't you play your instrument for us right now?' Does that sound like fun to you?"

It did, actually. Of course, Riley didn't have any relatives who came over. And his mother didn't own a video camera.

And he wouldn't have an instrument.

"I want to do the flute," Sophie said. "I already play violin and piano, violin since I was four, piano since I was five. But it's not too late to add flute."

Erika wasn't looking at any of the instruments.

"Don't you want to be in band?" Riley asked her.

"Drums," Erika said. "I want to do drums. And I don't see any drums."

Mr. Simpson heard her. "They were too hard to transport today. But you can definitely play drums if you'd like. The percussion section is the heartbeat of the band."

Riley could picture Erika pounding away on drums.

"What about you?" Erika asked Riley then. He wasn't looking at the instruments, either. What was the point of falling in love with something you couldn't have? "Don't you want to do an instrument?"

"I guess not," Riley said.

———

"Did you get your homework done?" Riley's mom asked him as they drove out of the school parking lot at five-thirty. Because his mom had to work, Riley went to the after-school day care program in the gym.

"Sort of." He had done his spelling, but not his math homework, since he couldn't find the math worksheet. It was odd how quickly a math worksheet could disappear into thin air.

He thought of another title for his biography: *Riley O'Rourke: The Boy Who Made Homework Disappear*. It would be a best seller, Riley was sure of it.

Or *Riley O'Rourke: The Boy Who Didn't Get to Play the Saxophone*.

It probably wasn't even worth asking, but he made himself do it. "Can we rent a saxophone?" he blurted out.

"A saxophone?" She sounded as surprised as if he had asked for a pet elephant.

Riley explained to her about instrumental music. "But you have to rent an instrument. And Mr.

Simpson said it costs twenty-five dollars a month."

She didn't answer right away. That gave Riley a ray of hope.

"It's a lot of money," she said slowly. "But it isn't just the money. You're having a hard enough time with your schoolwork as it is. It takes you forever to get your homework done. I can't see adding another distraction. And you know how you lose things. What if we paid all that money to rent a saxophone, and you lost it?"

Riley wouldn't lose it. Some things you didn't lose. You just didn't.

They pulled into the parking space in front of their apartment.

"Anyway," Riley's mother said, "we really can't afford it, honey. I wish we had the money for extras, but we don't. So there's no point in worrying about it."

3

Dinner was macaroni and cheese, the good kind that came in a box. Riley's mom made him eat some broccoli with it. Once he had asked her if she'd pay him for eating broccoli. She had laughed. So he still had to eat broccoli for free.

After dinner, Riley told his mother, "I have to go to the library."

"Tonight?"

"Well, sometime. I have to get a biography of Teddy Roosevelt by Friday." Riley told her about the biography tea.

"That sounds like so much fun!"

Her enthusiasm gave Riley an idea: the teachers and parents could go to the biography tea, while the kids played video games at Grant's house.

"Let's go tonight. I'm so proud of you for wanting to get a good start on this!"

What Riley really wanted to get a good start on was playing the saxophone, but he didn't say anything.

When they got to the library, Grant was there, too. Riley was surprised that Grant's mother hadn't taken him to the library the minute after school got out, at 3:01. But then he remembered that Grant had his soccer practice on Wednesdays.

Riley found a biography of Teddy Roosevelt right away. Unfortunately, there was no biography with exactly 100 pages. The best he could do was 127. Poor Grant's biography of Gandhi had 158 pages.

"Wait till you see the pictures," Grant warned him as they checked out their books.

The guy *was* bald! And he *was* wearing some kind of strange, white underwear-like thing.

"It's called a loincloth," Grant informed Riley. "I think it's child abuse to make a kid wear a loincloth."

Some of the pictures showed Gandhi wearing normal clothes, but Grant kept going back to the picture of Gandhi in the loincloth. Riley knew that Grant enjoyed making his project sound as terrible as possible, to upset his mom.

"Do you want me to go talk to Mrs. Harrow?" she asked.

"That's all right," Grant said, sounding noble. "Sometime in life everyone has to wear a loincloth. In public. To school. In front of the whole class."

Then Grant's face changed. "Look at that!"

Riley turned and saw Sophie coming into the library, led by her mother. Sophie was blindfolded.

"What on earth happened to Sophie?" Grant's mother asked.

Riley knew. "She's being Helen Keller." Sophie had known about the biography assignment for all of six hours, and already she was acting the part.

Both mothers chuckled. Then they headed off together to look at magazines.

"Hi, Sophie!" Grant called out in a fake high voice.

"Hi, Grant!" Sophie replied serenely.

"Hi, Sophie!" Riley called out in a low, growly voice.

"Hi, Riley."

Sophie was amazing.

"Helen Keller was blind *and* deaf," Grant pointed out, using his normal voice this time.

"I'm practicing being blind first," Sophie said. "Then I'll practice deafness. We stopped at the drugstore on the way here to buy earplugs."

"How are you going to find your biography if you can't see the computer catalog?" Grant wanted to know.

"My mother is going to help me. People helped Helen Keller, too, like her teacher, Annie Sullivan."

"Where did you learn so much about Helen Keller?" Riley asked. "You haven't even gotten your biography yet."

Sophie shrugged. "Everybody knows some things."

Riley felt as if he didn't know anything.

Riley's mother and Grant's mother hadn't returned yet. Sophie's mother was typing away at the computer catalog across the room.

"Let's play a trick on Sophie," Grant whispered.

"Like what?"

Grant got down on all fours and crawled over to Sophie's feet and started meowing. Riley set his book down to watch him.

"Very funny, Grant-the-cat."

Grant tried again. "Oh, Sophie, look! There's a snake crawling into the library. A long, slithery one."

"A snake in the library," Sophie said scornfully. "I suppose it just opened the door and came in all by itself?"

"Wait! There's a spider! A big black hairy one. It's coming right toward you!"

It was hard to tell what someone was thinking

when you couldn't see her eyes. But this time Sophie wasn't so quick with her response.

"I'm not afraid of spiders," she said uncertainly.

"There really *is* a spider!" Grant told her. "Honest! I wouldn't lie about something like that. I've never seen such a big one!" He reached out a hand and brushed Sophie's arm.

Sophie gave a muffled scream and tore off her blindfold. "Where is it? Where's the spider?"

Grant burst out laughing. Sophie glared at him with pure rage.

"If you were really Helen Keller, you wouldn't be able to take off your blindfold," Grant said.

"Well, if you were really Mahatma Gandhi, you wouldn't be playing stupid tricks on people."

"Guess what? I'm not really Mahatma Gandhi. Lucky me."

Sophie's mother came bustling over. "I found three biographies. I know you'll want the longest one. I'm glad you took off that blindfold, honey.

It's well and good to practice being Helen Keller, but a little bit of pretending goes a long way."

"I've practiced being blind enough for one day." Sophie swept off with her mother to the non-fiction stacks.

Riley wondered whether Teddy Roosevelt had ever played tricks on people. He didn't know anything about Teddy Roosevelt, except that he was President and had a mustache and had his head carved on Mount Rushmore.

Back at home, Riley thought he might look at the first page of his biography, to see how hard it was going to be. But where was it?

"I can't find my library book," Riley confessed.

"Oh, Riley. It has to be here somewhere."

Riley looked everywhere. He still couldn't find it.

"I think I left it at the library." He had a dim memory of laying it down on a table while Grant was meowing at Sophie.

"Oh, Riley," his mother said again. "The library's closed now. We'll have to go back tomorrow and hope it's still there. Do you see why I don't want to rent a saxophone?" She sounded tired and discouraged.

Riley felt tired and discouraged, too. He bet Teddy Roosevelt didn't forget everything. A person who forgot his own head if it weren't fastened on wouldn't get *his* head carved on Mount Rushmore.

4

During reading time on Fridays, Mrs. Harrow let her students sit anywhere they wanted: on the rug, in the beanbag chairs by the bookcases, even outside on days that were warm and sunny—anywhere but on the couch. Only the two special students who were the "couch potatoes" for the week were allowed to sit on the couch. The couch potato names were drawn from Mrs. Harrow's big papiermâché potato.

This week Riley was a couch potato.

Unfortunately, Erika was a couch potato, too.

If only Riley and Grant could have been couch potatoes together. But so far this year, Mrs. Harrow's potato had never picked best friends in the same week. Riley sometimes wondered if it was rigged.

Grant plopped down on the floor next to the couch, like a couch potato that had rolled onto the floor. A floor potato. The couch potatoes and the floor potato started reading.

Riley read slowly. There were a lot of hard words in his biography of Teddy Roosevelt, which he had brought home from the library yesterday. Words like *asthma*. When he was a little boy, Teddy Roosevelt had asthma. Asthma was a sickness that made it hard to breathe. When young Teddy had trouble breathing at night, his father would take him out for rides in his carriage.

Teddy Roosevelt was lucky to have a father, Riley thought.

And to be rich. The Roosevelts had piles and piles of money. If Teddy Roosevelt had wanted a saxophone, his father could have bought him one in a second.

But maybe, since Teddy had asthma, it would have been hard for him to blow into a saxophone.

Still, it was even harder blowing into a saxophone if you didn't have a saxophone—and were never going to have one.

At the other end of the couch, Erika slammed her book shut. Uh-oh. Grant looked up from his. Riley saw that Grant was already on chapter three.

"How's empire ruling?" Grant asked pleasantly.

A spot of red burned in each of Erika's cheeks. "It's Queen Elizabeth's father. Guess what he did."

Riley had no idea.

"He made her sit cross-legged in her underwear?" Grant suggested, even though Erika was clearly in no mood for jokes.

"Queen Elizabeth's father," Erika said, "cut off Queen Elizabeth's mother's head."

That was bad, all right. Maybe fathers weren't such a great thing—at least some of them.

"Why did he do that?" Grant asked.

Erika's eyes glittered with rage. "He did it because he was mad that Elizabeth wasn't a *boy*. He wanted a *boy*."

"That's awful," Riley said, so Erika would know

that he didn't agree with Queen Elizabeth's father *at all.*

"Maybe you should have kept Florence Nightingale," Grant suggested.

Ignoring Grant, Erika opened her book again.

"I guess she doesn't think she should have kept Florence Nightingale," Grant said.

"Be quiet," Erika snapped at him. "I want to find out what happens next."

"How's Gandhi?" Riley whispered to Grant.

"He's wearing normal clothes so far," Grant whispered back.

Riley returned to reading. Teddy's father told him that he would have to cure himself from being weak and sickly. He was going to have to *make* his body. So Teddy started lifting weights and pulling himself up on rings and bars. He asked to take boxing lessons and learned how to box.

Riley's thoughts wandered. What if he had a father who said, "Riley, you must *make* yourself into a saxophone player!" Then his father would buy him a brand-new saxophone, the way Mr. Roosevelt had built Teddy his own private gym. Just as Teddy Roosevelt had asked his father for boxing lessons, Riley would ask his father for sax lessons.

"Sure, son," he imagined his father saying with a proud grin. Riley practiced the proud grin.

"What are you smiling about?" Grant asked him.

The question pulled Riley back to reality.

"Nothing." He had no father, no sax, no lessons, no proud grin.

Riley wondered what Teddy Roosevelt would have done if he hadn't had a rich father who could give him anything he wanted. Riley was only up to page 19, but he already knew that if Teddy hadn't been given a gym, he would have built himself one. If he hadn't had weights to lift, he would have lifted chairs, or rocks, or bales of hay.

Unfortunately, there was no substitute for a saxophone. Teddy could lift anything and build strong muscles. Riley couldn't blow into just anything and make music.

But still. If Teddy Roosevelt had wanted a saxophone, he would have gotten himself a saxophone. Somehow.

Riley read another few pages. Teddy Roosevelt's father died! Riley felt sorry for Teddy Roosevelt even though he was just reading about him in a book. Teddy Roosevelt had been a real person, and everything in the book was true. Riley didn't have a father, and now Teddy Roosevelt didn't have a father, either. Riley and Teddy were the same.

Riley opened his language arts notebook—he had remembered to bring it to school that day!—and found a blank page halfway through.

Ways to Get a Saxophone, he wrote at the top of the page.

But he couldn't think of a single thing to write next. *Make one.* He couldn't make a saxophone. *Find one.* Like where? And if he found one, it would probably belong to someone else. "Finders keepers" didn't apply to saxophones. *Borrow one.* From whom? *Earn the money to get one.*

That idea didn't seem as dumb as all the rest.

It might even be, as Teddy Roosevelt would have said, a *bully* idea. According to Riley's book, *bully* meant "great, terrific, wonderful."

Earn the money to get one, Riley wrote on his page.

Of course, he didn't know how much money he'd have to earn, or how a nine-year-old kid could possibly go about earning it. And even if he did, his mother had said he shouldn't do instrumental music because he was having enough trouble getting his regular homework done.

Riley added to his list: *Do better on my homework so my mom will let me have one.*

"All right, class!" Mrs. Harrow called out. "Reading time is over. Go back to your desks and get out your math books."

Riley got off the couch. Erika shut her book with a bang. She must still be mad at Queen Elizabeth's father.

At least Riley had started a list. Step one was making a list of what to do.

But the harder part was step two: doing it.

5

On Saturday morning, Riley settled down on the couch to watch cartoons. He knew he should be reading his Teddy Roosevelt book, but he could learn about Teddy Roosevelt later.

Riley's mother clicked off the TV.

"Mom!"

She waved the newspaper at him. "We're going to yard sales."

Riley groaned, but his mother ignored him. She loved yard sales the way Grant loved video games, the way Mrs. Harrow loved biography teas. She loved yard sales the way Riley loved saxophones.

Reluctantly, Riley shoved his feet into his sneakers.

"We can look for items for your Teddy Roosevelt costume," his mother said. "What did Teddy Roosevelt wear?"

Riley checked the cover of his book. "A fringed jacket, and boots, and a hat, and a bandanna, and these weird glasses that sort of stick on your nose, and a mustache."

"Well, we can look, at least."

Riley imagined the ad in the newspaper:

HUGE YARD SALE!
Come buy glasses that stick on your nose!
Mustaches!

"Can Grant come, too?"

"I doubt Grant wants to spend his morning at yard sales."

But when Riley called him, Grant did want to go. "Better yard sales than working on my report or trying to figure out how to play my trumpet."

Grant's parents had already bought him a brand-new trumpet for instrumental music.

Sometimes Riley couldn't help feeling jealous of Grant.

"Maybe we can find some great-looking loin-cloths," Grant said.

Sometimes Riley *didn't* feel jealous of Grant.

The first yard sale had lots of baby things: a crib, a stroller, piles of tiny clothes. It had adult clothes, too, but nothing Teddy Roosevelt or Mahatma Gandhi would have worn. No mustaches, no loincloths.

The next yard sale had a whole table full of used video games. Grant had them all. Riley didn't have any of them. But he wasn't going to spend his money on video games. Not if he could save it to buy himself a saxophone. He had five dollars and fifty cents crammed into his pocket right now.

The man at the third yard sale looked familiar. Riley was sure he was somebody's dad from school. Then a woman came out of the house. It was Sophie's mother.

"Let's go," Riley said. "There's no good stuff here."

"We haven't even gotten out of the car yet!" Riley's mom protested. "And look! There's Sophie's mom. You boys can chat with Sophie if you don't see anything that interests you."

Luckily, Sophie was nowhere to be seen. Maybe she was at the library, filling out her seven hundredth note card on Helen Keller.

Riley and Grant started looking at the sale tables. Sophie had an older brother, so there might be something worth buying, after all. Grant found a video game he didn't have and almost fainted with joy. Riley found a red bandanna that cost a quarter. Now all he needed was the jacket, the boots, the hat, the glasses, and the mustache.

Then, next to a stack of old *National Geographic* magazines, Riley found something that made his heart race. It was a book of music. Saxophone music. Alto saxophone music for the beginner.

Riley stared at the book. *Where there's saxophone music, there must be a saxophone.*

"Hi, Grant. Hi, Riley." It was Sophie. Apparently her seven hundred index cards were filled out already.

Grant held up his video game. "Hey, Sophie, how come your brother turned out normal?"

Sophie didn't react.

Grant tried again. "How come he turned out normal when you're so strange?"

Sophie just smiled. Grant looked puzzled. Then Sophie pointed to her ears. "I have my earplugs in. I'm practicing being deaf today. So far it's a lot easier than being blind. For one thing, I don't have to listen to any dumb comments from boys."

But how was Riley going to ask her about the saxophone if she couldn't hear? Not that he had the nerve to ask.

Sophie's mother came over to the table. "Are you boys finding anything?"

It was now or never. "Um."

That was as far as Riley got. He pointed to the saxophone music.

"I think the price on that is marked. Yes, it's twenty-five cents."

Riley had a quarter. But what good was saxophone music without a saxophone?

"You don't have . . . You aren't selling . . ."

Grant drifted off to another table, and then Riley whispered, "A saxophone?"

Instantly Grant whirled around. "A saxophone? What do you want a saxophone for?"

Riley's mother, browsing at the next table, gave him a worried look. "But, Riley, I thought we said . . ."

Sophie's mother hesitated. "Jake isn't playing his sax anymore. I'll ask him if he wants to sell it." She hurried inside.

"You *want* to do instrumental music?" Grant asked.

Riley nodded.

"What about your homework, Riley?" his mother asked gently. "We've already talked about this, remember?"

"If I can do saxophone, I'll study harder. I'll study three hours a day." *Well, two.* "I'll get all B's." *Well, C's.* "I'll do the best I can. I will. I promise." That much was true.

Riley's mom's face softened. "Well, *if* it doesn't cost too much, and *if* you truly promise to apply yourself to your schoolwork, I'll let you do instrumental music."

Sophie's mother came back out of the house, carrying a saxophone case. She set it on the grass next to Riley. He wanted to reach down and touch it, but he didn't.

"It's practically brand-new," Sophie's mother said. "I could let you have it for . . ."

Five dollars! Five dollars and fifty cents!

"A hundred dollars, I guess."

"I'm sorry," Riley's mother said. She sounded sorry, too, sorrier than Riley had heard her sound about anything for a long time. "That's too much for us right now."

Riley wasn't going to cry, he wasn't. Teddy Roosevelt wouldn't cry. Teddy's first wife died, and he came in last in his election for mayor of New York City, but he didn't cry. He kept on trying.

"Do you still want the sax music?" Sophie's mother asked.

Riley almost shook his head.

Then slowly he pulled out his two quarters, one for the bandanna, one for the music book.

One bandanna didn't make you Teddy Roosevelt.

One used music book didn't make you a musician.

But at least it was a start.

6

"I need to go to the library again," Riley told his mother the next Saturday.

"Oh, Riley, you didn't lose that biography, did you?"

"No!" Riley said indignantly. He really was getting better. He had finished reading the whole entire biography of Teddy Roosevelt, and he had twenty index cards already. *And* he had found a great stick-on mustache at the downtown costume store for just seventy-nine cents.

That meant he had seventy-nine cents less in his saxophone fund. Maybe he could sell his mustache after the biography tea, if there was still enough sticky stuff left on the back.

"So why do you need to go to the library?" his mother asked.

"Mrs. Harrow wants us to look at three other sources for our report. Like encyclopedias. Or the Internet. I can take the bus if you don't want to drive me." The public bus ran every ten minutes between Riley's house and downtown; kids under ten could ride for free.

His mother hesitated. She was curled up on the couch, reading the newspaper in her pajamas. "If Grant goes with you, I suppose you'll be all right. Just pay attention to where your stop is. And check that you don't leave anything on the bus."

"Mom! I won't leave anything. All I'm taking is my envelope of note cards."

"It never hurts to check," she said.

It was fun riding the bus with Grant, sitting in the backseat, arguing about who got to pull the cord when it was time to get off. When Riley pulled it at their stop, he felt grownup enough to be in middle school.

At the library, they saw lots of other kids from school: Harriet Tubman, Martin Luther King, Jr., Louisa May Alcott—and Helen Keller.

"You're not done with your note cards yet?" Grant asked. "I don't believe it."

Sophie smiled. Riley saw she was wearing her earplugs. Then she made strange motions with her hands. She must be learning sign language.

"What did you say?" Riley asked. He had a feeling that it was some kind of insult about boys.

Grant made his own series of hand movements in return. Sophie looked puzzled.

"Do you know sign language, too?" Riley asked him.

"Nope," Grant said cheerfully. "But that meant girls are dumb, and girls wearing earplugs and pretending to be Helen Keller are the dumbest of all."

This time Sophie glared at him. She must not be as deaf as she seemed. Or maybe she could read lips. That was probably it. In a week of practice, Sophie had already become a champion lip-reader.

Riley found the encyclopedias and looked up Roosevelt, Theodore. The entry didn't tell Riley anything new, but Mrs. Harrow thought it was important to double-check all facts. Teddy Roosevelt became a Rough Rider and charged up San Juan Hill during the Spanish-American War. He was elected Vice President of the United States, and then became President when William McKinley was assassinated. He decided to dig the Panama Canal. He created 150 national forests and 5 national parks.

Riley filled ten new note cards. His favorite told about the hikes Teddy Roosevelt used to take with his children. Their goal was to go over or through all obstacles along the way, but never around them. If they came to a rock, they had to climb right over it. If they came to a river, they had to jump in and start swimming.

How would that apply to getting a saxophone? Riley thought about Sophie's brother's sax. It was easier to climb over a huge rock or cross a raging river than to come up with one hundred dollars when all a person had was four dollars and twenty-one cents.

"Are you ready to go?" Grant asked him.

"Sure." Riley collected his cards, stuffed them in his envelope, and followed Grant out the door. "What's Gandhi up to these days?"

"Well, it's actually pretty amazing," Grant said slowly. "The guy was, like, really brave. He would never use violence against anybody, no matter how much violence they used against him. There was this unfair British law against collecting salt."

"*Salt?*"

"I know, it sounds dumb, but that's what it was. Gandhi and his followers marched all the way to the sea, hundreds of miles, to collect salt, and the British kept attacking them, but they didn't fight back, they just kept on going."

"Wow," Riley said. They had reached the bus stop. "What about the underwear? Why did he dress like that?"

"He wanted to be poor and simple. And not wear any clothes made by the British."

"So what are you going to wear to the biography tea?"

Grant stared at him. "What do you think? If

I'm going to do this thing, I'm going to do it right. But I'll wear my swimsuit underneath."

On the bus ride home, the bus driver had a perfect Teddy Roosevelt mustache. Riley and Grant sat in the back of the bus again and talked more about loincloths.

"You'd have to wear a lot of sunblock all the time in the summer," Riley said.

"Yeah, and in the winter you'd need a coat or something. A swimsuit underneath and a coat on top."

This time Grant pulled the cord for their stop.

The instant Riley got off the bus, he had a terrible feeling. "My note cards! I left them on the bus!" He watched in disbelief as the bus rumbled away.

"The envelope's not in your pockets?"

Just to be sure, Riley patted his pockets, but he knew his cards were on the bus.

Thirty note cards. A whole week of work. Everything he needed for his five-page paper. Gone. Forever.

No. *Not* gone forever. If Teddy Roosevelt lost his index cards for a book report, he'd get them back. This was just another obstacle to climb over.

Riley tried to stay calm. There was no way that he could catch up with the bus, however fast he ran after it.

"If we wait for the next bus," Riley said, thinking out loud, "maybe that driver can call this driver and tell him I left my cards. And then he can stop on the way back and give them to me."

"What if someone stole them?" Grant asked.

"Who's going to steal index cards for a report on Teddy Roosevelt?"

"Someone else writing a report on Teddy Roosevelt?"

Riley punched him in the shoulder.

"Okay," Grant said. "I'll wait with you."

As they waited, the wind came up. A few drops of rain fell. Riley and Grant huddled under a tree. It seemed a lot longer than ten minutes, but finally the bus appeared. As soon as the door wheezed open, Riley blurted out his problem.

The driver sighed. "I can't be bothering another driver about some kid's note cards."

"Please?" Riley begged. "*Thirty* note cards? For a *five*-page paper? On Teddy *Roosevelt*?"

The driver sighed again. "Okay. But next time, check your seat before you get off the bus."

Riley was glad his mother wasn't there to hear him say it.

Two more buses went by as Riley stood shivering under the tree, glad that Grant had stayed by his side. Riley looked at each driver to see if he had a Teddy Roosevelt mustache.

Half an hour later, a bus appeared at the stop, driven by a man with the right kind of mustache. Riley waited breathlessly while the door opened.

Grinning, the driver presented Riley with his envelope of note cards.

"Thank you!" Riley said, clutching it tightly.

"No problem," the driver said. "One time a lady left her kid on the bus. Had four kids with her, and got off with three. That was worse."

Worse for the driver, maybe, and for the lady, but not for Riley.

Thirty note cards found! One raging river crossed!

Now all Riley needed was a saxophone.

7

The next day, Riley worked on a list of ways that a fourth grader could earn money.

1. Mow lawns.

But he lived in an apartment complex where all the lawns were mowed by a lawn-mowing company.

2. Shovel snow.

It was only September. And when it did snow, all the walks where he lived would be shoveled by a snow-shoveling company.

3. Walk dogs.

His apartment complex didn't allow pets.

It was hard to earn money when you lived in an apartment. It was hard for a fourth grader to earn money, period.

Riley called Grant. Grant always had lots of ideas. "I need to earn some money to buy that saxophone."

"Too bad you don't want a trumpet. I'd sell mine cheap. If I could sell it without my parents finding out. Which I can't."

Riley had an idea of his own just then. "Maybe I could have a yard sale. Like Sophie's."

For a moment, he was excited. Then he remembered. He and his mom didn't have a yard. And he and his mom had nothing to sell.

"We could have one together," Grant suggested. "I've been thinking. I don't really need all my old video games."

Riley almost fell off his chair. He made a small, strangled sound of surprise into the phone.

"Well, I don't. I mean, it's not like Gandhi had dozens of video games. He didn't even have *pants*. I don't play with half of my games anymore, anyway. My mom'd be thrilled if I got rid of them."

"But what would *I* sell?"

If Grant sold his video games, Grant would make money, not Riley. And Grant didn't need the money, Riley did.

"You could help me with the sale, like make the signs or something, and we could split the money," Grant offered.

Riley's heart soared. "Do you mean it?"

"Sure. It'll be the video game sale of the century."

That week, Grant and Riley told everyone at school about their yard sale. And Riley spent all Friday evening making signs on pieces of cardboard cut up from discarded cartons he found in the recycling bin, while jazz music blared on the radio.

GREAT VIDEO GAME SALE

EVERYTHING MUST GO!

"Everything doesn't really need to go," Riley explained to his mother. "That's just a thing people put on yard sale signs."

First thing on Saturday morning, Riley biked around Grant's neighborhood, putting up the signs, while Grant organized the games on two tables in his front yard. Grant's mom donated free cookies and lemonade.

To Riley's amazement, their first customer was Erika. She rode up on her bike in queenly fashion. Riley wondered if she'd arrive at the biography tea wearing an old-fashioned dress, with one of those ruffly things around her neck, like Queen Elizabeth wore in pictures. He couldn't imagine Erika wearing a ruffly thing *or* a dress.

"I love video games," Erika announced. She started sorting through the first pile.

"There are no queens in any of them," Grant pointed out apologetically.

"That's okay," Erika said. "It's not that much fun being a queen."

Grant and Riley exchanged glances.

"You know how I told you that Queen Elizabeth's father beheaded Queen Elizabeth's mother? Well, when she was grown up, Queen Elizabeth

had her one true love, the Earl of Essex, beheaded. She had to do it for political reasons. But it broke her heart to do it."

Riley bet it didn't bother her one millionth as much as it bothered the Earl of Essex.

Kids from school trickled in throughout the morning. Toward lunch, Sophie came with her mother and her brother. Sophie wasn't wearing a blindfold or earplugs.

"Do you have anything besides video games?" Sophie asked as her brother greedily pawed through the remaining piles on the table.

"A trumpet," Grant said hopefully.

Sophie turned toward her mother. "Can I get a trumpet? I'd love to be able to play piano, violin, flute, *and* trumpet."

"I was just kidding," Grant told her. Sophie looked disappointed.

Riley remembered a question he had been meaning to ask Sophie. "How could Helen Keller use sign language if she couldn't see the signs?"

"Her teacher did the motions in her hand," Sophie explained. "And for reading books, she used Braille. She learned to talk, too, but that was really hard, because she could never hear what she sounded like."

Sophie straightened the pile of games her brother had been looking through. She straightened the pile of game magazines, too. "Everything was hard for Helen Keller," she said.

Riley thought about that for a minute. Lots of things had been hard for Teddy Roosevelt. And for Queen Elizabeth, and for Gandhi.

Maybe nobody's life was easy. At least, nobody who got to be the star of a biography. *Riley O'Rourke: The Boy Who Had No Problems Whatsoever*. Who would want to read that one? "Obstacles overcome" was one of the main topics Mrs. Harrow wanted them to include in their reports. Without that, the reports would be pretty boring.

Of course, one of the biggest obstacles in Riley's life right now was writing a report about the obstacles in Teddy Roosevelt's life. He grinned. But his report, all five pages of it, was almost ready for him to hand in on Wednesday.

Riley had spent every single afternoon during the week organizing his note cards, making his outline, and writing his rough draft. Then he had thought of a few things he wanted to change, and he had written the whole thing over again. All he had left to do was copy it once more in his best cursive—and prepare to face the biography tea on Friday.

Sophie's brother bought five games. He was their best customer.

When the sale was over, Grant and Riley counted the money together: thirty-six dollars.

"So . . ." Riley did the math in his head. "Eighteen dollars each!"

It wasn't enough for Sophie's brother's saxophone, but it was eighteen dollars more than Riley had had three hours ago.

"You can have the whole thing," Grant said. He shoved the pile of crumpled dollar bills, quarters, dimes, and nickels toward Riley.

"But—" Riley protested. It was too much.

"Go ahead, take it." Grant smiled. "Look, I'm poor and simple, right? I don't even have a pocket in my loincloth to put the money in."

Riley swallowed a lump in his throat. He was lucky to be friends with Mahatma Gandhi.

"Thanks," he said.

8

On the day of the biography tea, Riley studied himself in the mirror.

Bandanna around neck. Check.

Eyeglasses. His mother had found an old pair and taken the glass out of the frames. Check.

Broad-brimmed hat. Grant had one that Riley had borrowed. Check.

No leather jacket. That had been impossible to find. But Riley looked suitably rugged in jeans and a plaid flannel shirt. Check.

Carefully, Riley peeled off the tape from the sticky back of his mustache and pressed the mustache between his nose and his upper lip.

Check.

"Bully!" Riley pronounced. It was cool to look

in the mirror and see Teddy Roosevelt looking back at him.

"Are you ready to head off to school, Teddy?" his mother asked, giving him a hug.

Riley grinned. "Charge!" He felt ready to head off to the White House.

On the playground, Riley saw some other kids already in costume. Napoleon swaggered around in a navy-blue military uniform. Pocahontas was wearing a brown fringed tunic with matching leggings; her hair hung in two long dark braids.

Helen Keller had on an old-fashioned dress, but she wasn't blind or deaf yet. Riley wondered if Sophie would use a blindfold and earplugs all afternoon long, or just pretend. Either way, it would be interesting to see.

Queen Elizabeth was in her usual jeans and T-shirt, but she carried a large shopping bag, stuffed with something made of bright purple velvet.

Grant, too, showed up in regular clothes, with a much smaller shopping bag in hand.

"Is it in there?" Riley asked.

"One super-duper, deluxe, premium-grade loin-cloth. I'm not going to put it on until after lunch. My mom thought it would be too distracting."

Riley thought Grant's mom was probably right. You could forget you were wearing a mustache if you didn't happen to catch a glimpse of your reflection somewhere. But there was no way that you could forget you were wearing a loin-cloth. Or that anyone would let you forget.

The morning dragged. Teddy Roosevelt would have done long division with gusto—he did everything with gusto—but it was hard when the answer to the problem on the board was 324, with a remainder of 7, and Riley came up with 410, with a remainder of 8. He'd have to work harder on his math homework if he was going to get to buy Sophie's brother's saxophone. With the yard sale profits, he had $40.21 now. He was almost halfway there.

Finally, after lunch, Mrs. Harrow sent the kids who weren't in costume to the restrooms to change. The others sat at their desks and waited.

When Queen Elizabeth appeared, a ripple of astonishment ran through the classroom. There she stood, in an extremely fancy, long, purple-velvet, olden-days gown, with a crisp, stiff ruff around her neck. A crown sat on her newly red hair—a wig, Riley guessed. In her right hand she held a royal scepter.

Riley almost leaped to his feet to bow, but he stopped himself in time.

"What's happening? Who came in?" Sophie asked Riley. She had her blindfold on, but not her earplugs. Riley was glad Sophie wasn't trying to be blind and deaf simultaneously. Maybe she would alternate: blind for thirty minutes, deaf for thirty minutes.

"Erika has a great Queen Elizabeth outfit," Riley told her.

"Does she have a crown?"

"A crown *and* a wig. And she's carrying a scepter."

Sophie clicked her teeth in frustration. Riley

understood. It was one thing to be blind while doing homework at the library. It was another thing to be blind at the biography tea.

Socrates entered, looking embarrassed in a toga. Marie Curie bustled by in a lab coat.

"Has anyone seen Grant?" Mrs. Harrow asked Shakespeare and Isaac Newton, who had just emerged from the boys' room in their costumes. "He's the only one we're still missing."

"He's coming," Shakespeare said. Isaac Newton gave a chuckle that came out sounding more like a snort.

Riley flipped through his note cards one last time. He wanted to have all his facts straight in case anyone asked Teddy Roosevelt any hard questions.

Suddenly the room exploded into shrieks of laughter. Riley looked up, startled.

Mahatma Gandhi had entered.

In a loincloth.

And completely bald.

"Grant!" Mrs. Harrow cried out.

"The name is Gandhi. Mahatma Gandhi."

"Your hair!"

"I shaved it off. I brought in my dad's electric razor and plugged it into an outlet in the boys' room."

"Do your parents know about this?" Mrs. Harrow asked faintly.

Grant nodded. "I told them I needed to do it to get an A. So do I get an A?"

Mrs. Harrow visibly pulled herself back together. "The grade for our biography unit is based on the written report, which I'll hand back in a minute, and on the costume, and on how well you act as your character at the tea party. But for your costume today, yes, you get an A."

Riley felt a tiny bit hurt that Grant hadn't told him about his head-shaving plan. But he also felt glad that he had the coolest best friend of anyone.

Most of all, he felt nervous about his grade on the report. His mother would never let him do instrumental music if he ended up with a C or a D. But if he got a B—or even better than a B . . .

71

"All right, class," Mrs. Harrow said. "I'll give you your reports, and then we'll move into the library, where our room mothers have set up for our tea party."

She handed back the reports in alphabetical order. Grant got his before Riley.

"A," he signaled to Riley.

Mrs. Harrow laid Riley's report on his desk. He could hardly bear to make himself look at the grade at the end, but he did.

A–!

Mrs. Harrow had written, "Great job, Riley! Lots of interesting details, especially about the Roosevelt family's hikes. Next time, check your spelling." It was the best grade Riley had gotten on a report, ever.

"I can't see my grade!" Sophie wailed when Mrs. Harrow placed Sophie's report on her desk.

As if Sophie needed to look to know she had gotten an A+.

Riley's own A– made him feel generous. "Do you want me to look for you?" he offered.

She hesitated. "Okay."

Riley peeked. "A-plus."

Sophie sighed with satisfaction. "Thanks, Riley."

"Hey," Riley said, since Sophie was being so friendly. "I have over forty dollars saved up so far, to buy your brother's saxophone."

She didn't reply.

"The one I saw at your yard sale?" Riley said, to remind her.

With her blindfold on, Riley couldn't see Sophie's eyes. But her mouth looked stricken. "He already sold it," Sophie said.

"No!" Riley couldn't believe it. His one best chance at a sax, gone just like that.

"Two days ago. I didn't know you were saving up for it. I'm so sorry, Riley."

9

"Famous authors, artists, inventors, generals, presidents, kings, queens, and all you contributors to the culture and civilization of our world," Mrs. Harrow said in a grand voice, "please follow me to the library for our biography tea."

Numb, Riley stood up. He wasn't Teddy Roosevelt anymore, just a kid who didn't have a saxophone and would never have one.

"Ow!" Sophie cried out crossly as she banged her shin into a chair. "I hate being blind!"

"I hate wearing a loincloth," Grant said, but Riley didn't think he meant it. Grant still looked pretty pleased about the whole thing.

"I hate wearing a dress," Erika said. "If I really was a queen, the first thing I'd do is outlaw dresses."

To Riley's surprise, Erika took Sophie's arm and helped her walk in the procession to the library. Had she gotten nicer since becoming a queen?

Riley fell into step beside Grant. "Sophie told me her brother just sold his sax," Riley said, trying to keep his voice steady.

"Bummer," Grant said.

It was more than a bummer. It was the worst thing that had happened to Riley since his dad left five years ago. "So where am I supposed to get a saxophone now?" This time his voice did wobble.

"We'll think of something," Grant said. "Mahatma and Teddy will think of something."

Riley felt like giving up instead.

All the tables in the library were covered with white tablecloths and set with china plates, cups, and saucers; stiff cloth napkins; and forks and spoons that gleamed like real silver. On each table stood a vase full of flowers, and two teapots. Every teapot was different. Riley saw one shaped like a

little house and one shaped like a black-and-white cow.

"Look for your name cards," Mrs. Harrow instructed them.

Riley searched for his. He was at a table with Gandhi, Queen Elizabeth, Napoleon, Abraham Lincoln, and Queen Victoria.

"I thought the six of you might enjoy talking politics," Mrs. Harrow said as she stopped at their table to pour tea.

One of their teapots was fat and round and yellow; the other was shaped like Humpty Dumpty. Several of the mothers were going from table to table with plates of small sandwiches, pastries, and cut-up fruit. Sophie's mom was there helping, but Grant's mom and Riley's mom had to be at work.

"So, Queen Victoria," Grant said to Mandy, the girl who was dressed up as Queen Victoria. "You conquered India to add it to the British Empire, but I liberated it."

Queen Victoria scowled. Maybe it wasn't the best idea to talk politics.

What else could they talk about? All Riley wanted to talk about was how to get a saxophone. But he couldn't very well ask Mahatma Gandhi, Abraham Lincoln, Queen Elizabeth, Queen Victoria, or Napoleon.

Or could he?

"I have a question," Riley said.

"Yes, Teddy?" Queen Elizabeth said.

"Well, it's not really a Teddy Roosevelt question. It's just a question. If you wanted something more than anything in the world, and you didn't have the money to buy it, how would you get it?"

"Conquer it," said Napoleon.

"I guess I could behead anyone who wouldn't give it to me," Queen Elizabeth said, "but that gets old after a while."

"I'd go on a hunger strike until someone gave it to me," Gandhi said, stuffing a huge cookie in his mouth.

"I'd write a speech about it," Abraham Lincoln said. "Four score and seven years ago, I wanted this thing."

Queen Victoria appeared to be thinking. "It would depend on what kind of thing it was," she said wisely. "What would you do, Teddy?"

What *would* Teddy do? Riley sighed. "I'd keep on working and working and never give up."

Riley was no closer to knowing what to do than he had been before. Conquering, beheading, going on hunger strikes, giving speeches—those weren't really helpful suggestions. Working hard was helpful, sort of. But Riley had already worked so hard. He had worked hard enough on his Teddy Roosevelt report to get an A–. He had worked hard with Grant on the yard sale to earn $36. What was he supposed to do now? He could ask his mom again, but he had heard her complaining about bills just the other day.

Suddenly from Sophie's table there came a deafening crash. It was followed by a piercing scream. Riley could see a teapot—a pink one with red roses all over it—shattered on the floor. An enormous pool of tea was spreading everywhere.

Sophie jumped up from the table and yanked off her blindfold.

"I can't do it!" she cried. "I can't be blind. Helen Keller was blind *and* deaf, but I can't be blind even for one hour!"

Sophie's mother gave her a hug as the other mothers scurried to get paper towels to soak up the tea and sweep up the teapot pieces.

"It's hard," Mrs. Harrow told Sophie. "Being Helen Keller is hard. But, Sophie, no one expected you to really *be* blind this afternoon, at our tea. We expected you to pretend. We're all just pretending, you know."

Riley was pretending most of all. He wasn't Teddy Roosevelt any more than Sophie was Helen Keller. He couldn't charge up a hill in a war, or be elected President, or dig the Panama Canal. He couldn't even get himself a saxophone so he could do fourth-grade instrumental music.

Maybe he should rip off his mustache, the way Sophie had ripped off her blindfold. Maybe he, too, should shout out, "I can't do it! I give up!"

He must have looked as bad as he felt, because Queen Elizabeth said to him in her new kind voice, "What's wrong, Teddy?"

Riley couldn't keep it inside any longer. "I don't have a saxophone."

Queen Elizabeth looked genuinely puzzled. "Did Teddy Roosevelt want to play the saxophone?"

"No! But I do. Me. Riley O'Rourke."

Riley could tell she still didn't understand. "So—can't you get a saxophone?"

"No!" He was in so deep now, he might as well admit the whole thing. "I don't have the money to get one. I've been working and saving, and I still don't have enough."

Gandhi reached over and patted him on the shoulder.

"I wish I could help you," Queen Elizabeth said, while Napoleon, Lincoln, and Queen Victoria looked on, gaping. "Queen Elizabeth was a pa-troness of the arts, you know. I helped Shake-speare, and now I want to help you."

"Help me how?" Riley didn't know if he felt nervous or hopeful. Probably both.

But he didn't want Queen Elizabeth getting him a saxophone. He wanted to get one himself. The Teddy Roosevelt way.

Not that it hurt to have a queen on your side.

"I want to help, too," Grant said.

It didn't hurt to have a brave bald guy in a loin-cloth on your side, either.

"Let's come up with a plan," Riley said.

10

"Maybe," Riley said, "I should talk to Mr. Simpson." He didn't know why he hadn't thought of that before. But he hadn't had an A– on a report before, either.

He could hear the sound of fifth-grade instrumental music coming down the hall from the cafeteria. The fifth graders had started already; the fourth graders were starting next week.

"That's a wonderful idea," Erika said.

It felt good being praised by a queen.

Erika went up to Mrs. Harrow and whispered something to her.

"Now?" Mrs. Harrow asked, looking displeased.

Erika whispered something else. Mrs. Harrow

hesitated. Then she smiled. "Certainly, Your Majesty," Riley heard her say.

Back at the table, Erika tapped Riley on the shoulder. "We're going to talk to Mr. Simpson."

"Now?" Riley sounded like Mrs. Harrow and not at all like Teddy Roosevelt. "I mean, now!"

Grant jumped up. "I'm coming, too. This'll be like the salt march to the sea. I'm good at salt marches."

Mrs. Harrow was busy at another table, so nobody stopped Grant as he followed Riley and Erika out the door.

In the hall, they met Sophie, coming back from the girls' room, where she had gone to calm down after breaking the teapot. She wasn't wearing a blindfold anymore; Riley could see that her eyes were red from crying. She wasn't wearing earplugs, either. Just her old-fashioned dress. It suited her better than regular clothes somehow.

She said something to them with her hands. "That means 'hi.' "

"Hi," Riley replied.

"Where are you three going?"

Riley explained.

"Can I come, too? Teachers always like me . . ."

But Sophie sounded uncertain. "I *think* they like me," she said. "Except when I break teapots."

"Hey, it was an accident," Grant said.

"I broke the prettiest one. The pink one with the rosebuds. I helped my mom set up for the tea after school yesterday, when I wasn't wearing a blindfold, and that teapot was the prettiest one. And now it's ruined forever."

Well, it was definitely ruined forever. There was no way it could be glued back together.

"Everyone makes mistakes," Riley said.

"I don't!" Sophie said. "At least, I didn't." Her voice was getting smaller and smaller.

"Look," Erika said crisply, "the teapot is broken. It can't be mended. Period. The end. Do you want to come with us to talk to Mr. Simpson, or not?"

It was a relief to Riley to hear her sounding cross again.

"I want to come," Sophie said. She gave Riley a shaky smile.

As they got close to the cafeteria, Riley could hear the fifth graders playing a lively march. It made him feel braver inside. Music could do that for you. It could change the way you felt. It could make everything better.

The four of them approached Mr. Simpson as the march soared to its end.

What if he said, "Why are you bothering me? I have no idea where you can get a saxophone. Stop wasting my time."

Instead he said, "What is this, Halloween a month early?"

Riley had forgotten that they were dressed in their biography-tea clothes: red hair, crown, mustache, bald head, loincloth, and all.

"I want to play the sax," Riley said. "And my mom can't afford to rent me an instrument. And I was working and saving to buy a second-hand sax—her brother's sax." He pointed at Sophie, who looked guilty and miserable again. "But he sold it

to someone else. And I got an A– on my Teddy Roosevelt report, so that proves I can do instrumental music and keep up with my other homework. So my mom will let me do it. But I don't have a sax."

There. He had said it.

"Does the school have any extra saxes that students can borrow?" Erika asked in her best queenly voice.

"Everyone needs to learn how to play an instrument," Sophie said. Riley waited for her to list the instruments that she played, but she didn't.

"Well, everyone who wants to," Grant added.

Mr. Simpson studied the four of them, as if still unsure why Queen Elizabeth, Teddy Roosevelt, Mahatma Gandhi, and some girl in an old-fashioned dress had shown up in the middle of his fifth-grade instrumental music class.

"So you want to play the sax," he said to Riley.

Riley nodded. His heart was in his throat.

"In that case," Mr. Simpson said, "welcome to instrumental music."

"So you *do* have a sax he can borrow?" Erika persisted.

"Of course I do. You kids are right. Everyone should have a chance to learn an instrument. The school district has a few used instruments it can loan out to students who need them. It just so happens that I have an extra sax in the back of my van right now."

Riley grinned.

Mr. Simpson tossed his car keys to Riley. "It's the dented van right by the back door. The sax sitting on the backseat is yours."

Five minutes later, Riley had returned Mr. Simpson's keys, and he and the others were back at the biography tea. Riley clutched the handle of his used, battered, beautiful case with his very own saxophone inside.

Now the title of his biography could be *Riley O'Rourke: The Boy Who Found a Way to Get Himself a Saxophone, After All.* Or maybe just *Riley O'Rourke: Sax Player.*

He gulped down a big sip of lukewarm tea,

careful not to drench his mustache. It tasted awful. Riley didn't care.

Mrs. Harrow beamed at him. "Congratulations," she said. "Bully for you, Teddy Roosevelt."

Gandhi lifted his teacup in a toast. At the next table, Helen Keller raised hers, too. And two queens, one president, and one emperor joined in.

Fun Facts About Theodore "Teddy" Roosevelt

- Sworn into office at age forty-two, Teddy Roosevelt was the youngest person in history to become president of the United States.

- Teddy Roosevelt was the first president to go up in an airplane, go down in a submarine, and ride in an automobile in public.

- In 1906, he became the first American to win the Nobel Peace Prize.

- In addition to being a politician and a naturalist, Teddy Roosevelt wrote and published numerous books.

- He was blind in one eye from a boxing accident that took place while he was in the White House.

- He once gave a full campaign speech immediately after being shot in the chest by a would-be assassin.

- As president, he created five national parks, including the Grand Canyon National Park, and eighteen national monuments.

- He often read three books in a single day. One of his favorite books to read to his children was *The Wind in the Willows*.

- And, of course, one of the most popular children's toys in the world is named after him: the teddy bear.

GOFISH

CLAUDIA MILLS

© Larry Harwood

What did you want to be when you grew up?
I always wanted to be a writer. The only other thing I even considered being was president of the United States. In third grade, I made a hundred-dollar bet with Jimmy Burnett that I would be president someday, but now I'm starting to think maybe Jimmy Burnett is going to win that bet.

When did you realize you wanted to be a writer?
When I was six and my sister was five, my mother gave each of us one of those marble composition notebooks. She told me that my notebook was supposed to be my poetry book, and she told my sister that her notebook was supposed to be her journal. So I started writing poetry, and my sister started keeping a journal, and we both found out that we loved doing it.

What's your most embarrassing childhood memory?

Oh, there are so many! One day in third grade, I decided to run away from school, and I made a very public announcement to that effect. But when I got to the edge of the playground, I realized I had no place to go, so I had to come slinking back again. That memory still makes me cringe.

What's your favorite childhood memory?

We vacationed every summer at a little lake in New Hampshire, and I remember sitting out on the lake in a rowboat, writing poems and drawing pictures and making up stories about imaginary princesses with my sister. Those were very happy days.

As a young person, who did you look up to most?

I mostly looked up to characters in books who were braver and stronger than I was, like Sara Crewe in *A Little Princess*, who loses her beloved father and has to live in poverty in Miss Minchin's cold, miserable garret, but never stops acting like the princess that she feels she is in inside. I also looked up to Anne of Green Gables for her spunk in breaking that slate over Gilbert Blythe's head.

What was your favorite thing about school?

It's sort of weird and nerdy to say this, but I loved almost everything about school, and during summer vacations, I'd even cross off the days until school started again. Best of all, I loved any writing assignments and being in plays. In fifth grade, I played the role of stuck-up cousin Annabelle in our classroom play of *Caddie Woodlawn*, and that was wonderful.

What was your least favorite thing about school?

Definitely PE! I was always terrible at PE. I just couldn't do any of the sports, and one time the fourth-grade teacher made the whole class stop and look over at how terribly I was doing this one exercise. I still hate her for that.

What was your first job, and what was your "worst" job?

My first job was working in the junior clothes department at Sears. Back then, three girls worked in one department: one to work the cash register, one to oversee the dressing room, and one to tidy up the clothes racks. I loved tidying up the clothes racks, buttoning up the dresses that needed buttoning. I loved buttoning one dress so much that I bought it, and then found that once I had it at home I had no desire to button it at all anymore. My worst job was being a waitress. I would have done all right if I could have handled just one table at a time, from drinks to salad to main course and then dessert, but my brain could not handle juggling all those different tables at once.

How did you celebrate publishing your first book?

I don't remember celebrating it. Now that I look back, I wish I had. It's a very special moment.

Where do you write your books?

I write all my books in longhand, lying on the couch, using the same clipboard-without-a-clip that I've had for thirty years, always using a white narrow-ruled pad with no margins, and always using a Pilot Razor Point fine-tipped black marker pen.

What sparked your imagination for *Being Teddy Roosevelt*?

When my boys (now all grown-up) were in elementary school, they both participated in the fifth-grade "biography tea," in which kids had to read a biography and attend a fancy tea party dressed up as that person. And my older son was, yes, Teddy Roosevelt.

At their real-life school, kids could choose the subject of their biographies, but I thought it would be more interesting to have kids in my book encounter great figures whose stories they might not otherwise have known. And so I have inattentive, dreamy Riley assigned to read about go-getting Teddy Roosevelt, and materialistic, video-game–playing Grant assigned to the very opposite figure of Mahatma Gandhi. Perfect Sophie gets assigned Helen Keller—as a child, I read Helen Keller's biography and was so inspired that I wrote Helen Keller a letter, only to find out she was already long dead! I also loved reading about Queen Elizabeth I, the subject of feisty Erika's report.

Finally, my younger son fell in love with the saxophone when he was Riley's age, and he is now a jazz studies major at the University of Colorado at Boulder.

Of the books you've written, which is your favorite?

I don't have a favorite. My books feel like my children; each one has such a huge piece of my heart in it. So I wouldn't want to hurt their feelings by loving one of them more than its brothers and sisters.

What challenges do you face in the writing process, and how do you overcome them?

By far the biggest challenge is learning how to accept, and even to welcome, criticism. I hate criticism and always want everybody to love my books from the very first draft. But the only way to grow as a writer, and to produce the best possible book, is to listen to what critical readers tell you, and then rewrite, rewrite, rewrite.

Which of your characters is most like you?

Each one is like me in some way, or maybe I become more like that character as I write about him or her. I think overall the two who are most like me are Dinah in the Dinah books and Lizzie in *Lizzie at Last*. Lizzie is so much like me that I even dedicated the book to myself: "For the girl I used to be."

What makes you laugh out loud?

I always laugh out loud if somebody is trying to do something in an oh-so-serious way and then something goes hideously and publicly awry. That kind of thing makes me howl.

What was your favorite book when you were a kid? Do you have a favorite book now?
It was and still is *Betsy and Tacy Go Downtown* by Maud Hart Lovelace, which I consider to be the finest novel in the English language.

If you could travel in time, where would you go and what would you do?
I'd go back to Amherst, Massachusetts, in the 1850s, and walk by Emily Dickinson's house, and see if she would lower a little basket out the window to me with a fresh-baked muffin and a freshly written poem in it.

What's the best advice you have ever received about writing?
Brenda Ueland says, in *If You Want to Write*, that writing is supposed to be fun, and that if we allow ourselves to let it be fun, stories and poems will just keep pouring out of us. I think she's right.

Do you ever get writer's block? What do you do to get back on track?
I don't, really. My secret is to write for a short, fixed time—usually an hour—every single day. That way I never get burned out from writing, and I never get far enough away from my story that I lose my momentum.

SQUARE FISH

What do you want readers to remember about your books?

I always try to have my main character learn a small but important truth about how to make his or her life better. Oliver learns that even if he can't change the whole world, he can change some little part of it. But I know when I think back to favorite books I read a long time ago, it tends to be some little, trivial-but-fun detail that sticks in my head.

What would you do if you ever stopped writing?

Oh, I hope I never do! But I do love reading almost as much, so I guess I'd just read, read, read. Or teach writing, which I do already and love doing.

What do you consider to be your greatest accomplishment?

I'm proud that I've written over forty books while always working full-time at another demanding profession (being a university professor of philosophy).

What would your readers be most surprised to learn about you?

My favorite food is candy, particularly seasonal candy: candy corn at Halloween, those little Conversation Hearts for Valentine's Day, Cadbury Creme Eggs at Easter.

R. W. ALLEY

What did you want to be when you grew up?

That depends on when the question got asked. In third grade, I wanted to be an astronaut or a clown. In sixth grade, I wanted to make puppets and put on shows. In middle school, I wanted to be a space explorer and make puppets. (I was done with the clown thing.) In high school, I wanted to fit in. In college, I thought I might be an art historian or make puppets and puppet movies. (The astronaut thing turned out to require some engineering skill and a strong stomach. It looked so much easier on TV.) Then one day, drawing a cartoon for the school newspaper, I thought, "Maybe I could do this for money." A wild notion, if you'd seen my drawings then.

I told my parents that I was going to be a lawyer.

When did you realize you wanted to be an illustrator?

The summer after college, I wrote and drew a story for fun. I thought it looked like a children's book, maybe. I showed it to a publisher and they bought it. It appeared that I had a career, or at least a job. The law would have to wait.

What's your first childhood memory?

Hard to tell. I've made up too many stories about what I seem to be thinking in my baby pictures.

What's your most embarrassing childhood memory?
(See above.)

What's your favorite childhood memory?
When it was very quiet on Saturday mornings, I'd sit at a little table in front of a small black-and-white TV and make clay figures and make up stories for them while I watched *Captain Kangaroo, Top Cat,* and *Fireball XL5*.

What was your worst subject in school?
Languages have always confused me.

What was your best subject in school?
History and English. My junior high and high school had no arts programs (visual or performing). It wasn't until college that I took an art class. I wasn't very good at it. I could never finish anything. I just kept doing the same project over and over.

What was your first job?
I sold televisions at a local department store. I was not gifted at sales. And the store is no more. Coincidence? You judge.

How did you celebrate publishing your first book?
I forgot to celebrate. I was in the middle of working on a second book.

Where do you work on your illustrations?
In a very nice room that used to be the garage but now has a tall bookcase with a rolling ladder.

Where do you find inspiration for your illustrations?
Everything around me provokes a visual idea. I love architecture and faces. I am always looking and trying

to remember what I see. A very useful skill for an illustrator.

Are you a morning person or a night owl?
I am a morning and a night person. I find the afternoon the most useless for working. Of course, this may be because I am sleepy.

What's your idea of the best meal ever?
Lobster in a restaurant beside the dock where the boat that earlier in the day hauled in the trap that caught my lobster is tied up.

Which do you like better: cats or dogs?
I like the loud variety of dogs and the quiet elegance of cats.

Where do you go for peace and quiet?
Inside my head

What makes you laugh out loud?
My children, my wife, most Monty Python and a good fart joke

What's your favorite song?
"Try to Remember" from the musical *The Fantasticks*

Who is your favorite fictional character?
Toad, Ratty, Mole, and Badger from *The Wind in the Willows*

What are you most afraid of?
A bad fart joke

What time of year do you like best?
No time of year. Time of day. Early morning and just before midnight.

What's your favorite TV show?
No favorite. None are that consistent.

If you were stranded on a desert island, who would you want for company?
My wife and children. Although, if we don't get a good cell signal, I'm not so sure about the children.

What's the best advice you have ever received about illustrating?
My advice has come from the drawings of the illustrators/artists I admire most: "Make it simple, make it clear, and don't overwork it."

What do you want readers to remember about your books?
Mostly, that they remember them.

What would you do if you ever stopped illustrating?
Do you know something I don't?

What do you consider to be your greatest accomplishment?
My children and a happy marriage

Where in the world do you feel most at home?
In my home

What do you wish you could do better?
Draw horses. I really stink at drawing horses. Also, shoes. Not so good on shoes.

What would your readers be most surprised to learn about you?
Next to lobster, I think an anchovy pizza is the best meal.

Frazzled by fractions, Wilson Williams keeps
his new math tutor a secret from everyone, even
his best friend, Josh. At least his pet hamster,
Pip, and a science fair project will help take his
mind off fractions. But will Wilson's secret
destroy his friendship?

Find out in
Fractions = Trouble!
by Claudia Mills.

1

Whenever Wilson Williams had a problem, he talked to his hamster, Pip. He had had Pip for only two weeks, but already she understood him better than anybody else in his family did.

"Multiplication was hard enough," Wilson told Pip on the first Saturday morning in April. "But now we have to do fractions."

Pip twitched her nose.

"Even worse, Mrs. Porter is giving us a huge test in three weeks."

Pip blinked.

"But that's not the worst thing."

Pip scampered across Wilson's bedspread. Luckily Wilson had his bedroom door closed so that she couldn't escape and get lost.

"Wait," Wilson said to Pip. "Don't you want to know what the worst thing is?"

He scooped up Pip and held her in both hands, facing him, as he leaned back against his pillow. Her bright little eyes really did look interested.

When Wilson had gotten Pip, her name had been Snuggles, but he had changed it to Pip, short for Pipsqueak. Pip's brother, Squiggles, was the classroom pet in Wilson's third-grade classroom.

"The worst thing," Wilson said, "is

that my parents are getting me a math tutor."

Pip's eyes widened with indignation.

"I know." Wilson set her down on his knee. Instead of scurrying away, she sat very still, gazing up at him sadly. But no amount of hamster sympathy could change that one terrible fact.

A math tutor! That meant Wilson would go to school and do fractions, and then after school he'd go see Mrs. Tucker and do more fractions. He'd have fractions homework for Mrs. Porter and more fractions homework for Mrs. Tucker.

And suppose his friends at school found out. Nobody else he knew had a math tutor. There were other kids who were bad at math. There were other kids who thought fractions were hard. There were even other kids who thought fractions were impossible. But Wilson had never heard of any other kid who had a math tutor.

Wilson picked up Pip again and stroked the soft fur on the top of her little head. Pip was the only good thing left in Wilson's life. From now on, the rest of his life was going to be nothing but fractions.

Wilson's best friend, Josh Hernandez, came over at two. As if Wilson's mother was sorry for not standing up for him at lunch, she took Kipper for a long bike ride so that the two older boys could play undisturbed.

Wilson didn't have a video game system, and he wasn't allowed to watch TV on playdates, so he and Josh tried to build the world's fastest race car with some junk in the garage. His dad made microwave popcorn, and Wilson and Josh had a contest for throwing popcorn up into the air and catching it in their mouths. Wilson won, with seven straight mouth catches to Josh's four. He began to feel more hopeful about his life.

"Do you have an idea for your science fair project yet?" Josh asked, after missing another popcorn catch. April was science fair month at Hill Elementary.

"Nope." Wilson had been too busy trying to talk his parents out of making him have a math tutor. "Do you?"

"Uh-huh."

Wilson could tell Josh was waiting for him to ask what it was. "What is it?"

"I have to warn you," Josh said. "It's not just a good idea, it's a great idea. Are you ready?"

Wilson nodded. He couldn't believe Josh thought his idea was so wonderful. Usually Josh thought everything was terrible.

"All right. Here it is. At what tempera-
ture does a pickle explode?"

Okay, Wilson had to admit, Josh's idea
was wonderful.

"You could do something about popcorn," Josh offered. "Who is better at catching popcorn in their mouths, boys or girls?
Or kids or grownups? Or dogs or cats? Or
kids or dogs? Or—"

Wilson shoved him good-naturedly. "I
get the idea."

"You could even thrill Mrs. Porter and
use fractions," Josh suggested. "Like: cats
catch half as much popcorn as dogs. Or
grownups catch half as much popcorn as
kids. Or—"

This time Wilson shoved Josh harder. It
was fine for Josh to joke about fractions.
Josh was pretty good at math.

Of course, to be fair to Josh, Josh didn't

know that Wilson was about to become the only kid in the history of Hill Elementary to have a math tutor.

Wilson was going to make sure that Josh never found out.

DISCOVER MORE HEARTWARMING TALES FROM

Claudia Mills

AVAILABLE FROM MACMILLAN CHILDREN'S PUBLISHING GROUP

"Mills writes with such a light, humorous touch that many scenes beg to be read aloud."—*Kirkus Reviews*

ISBN 978-0-312-67282-9
$5.99 US/$6.99 Can
How is Oliver supposed to change the world when his parents won't even let him do class projects on his own?

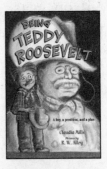

ISBN 978-0-312-64018-7
$5.99 US/$6.99 Can
Riley O'Rourke is researching President Teddy Roosevelt for the fourth-grade biography tea, but he has a more important goal: to get a saxophone.

ISBN 978-0-374-46452-3
$6.95 US/$6.95 Can
Third-grader Wilson struggles with his times tables in an attempt to beat the class deadline.

ISBN 978-1-250-00336-2
$5.99 US/$6.99 Can
In this sequel to *7 x 9 = Trouble!*, Wilson faces another mathematical challenge: fractions!

mackids.com